Dear Parents,

Welcome to the Scholastic Reader series. We have taken over 80 years of experience with teachers, parents, and children and put it into a program that is designed to match your child's interests and skills.

Level 1—Short sentences and stories made up of words kids can sound out using their phonics skills and words that are important to remember.

Level 2—Longer sentences and stories with words kids need to know and new "big" words that they will want to know.

Level 3—From sentences to paragraphs to longer stories, these books have large "chunks" of texts and are made up of a rich vocabulary.

Level 4—First chapter books with more words and fewer pictures.

It is important that children learn to read well enough to succeed in school and beyond. Here are ideas for reading this book with your child:

- Look at the book together. Encourage your child to read the title and make a prediction about the story.
- Read the book together. Encourage your child to sound out words when appropriate. When your child struggles, you can help by providing the word.
- Encourage your child to retell the story. This is a great way to check for comprehension.
- Have your child take the fluency test on the last page to check progress.

Scholastic Readers are designed to suppo~~~ ~~~ ~'s efforts to learn how to read at every age an~ ~~~ ~~~ ~oy helping your child learn to read ~~~ ~~~

—**Francie Alex**
   Chief Educatio.
   Scholastic Educ~

For Charlotte,
who will have many visits from the tooth fairy
—K.M.

For the kids at Camp Heartland
—M.S.

Text copyright © 2000 by Kate McMullan.
Illustrations copyright © 2000 by Mavis Smith.
Activities copyright © 2003 Scholastic Inc.
All rights reserved. Published by Scholastic Inc.
SCHOLASTIC, CARTWHEEL BOOKS, FLUFFY THE CLASSROOM GUINEA PIG,
and associated logos are trademarks and/or registered trademarks of Scholastic Inc.

Library of Congress Cataloging-in-Publication Data is available.

ISBN: 0-439-12918-4

17 16 15 14 13 12   10 11 12 13 14/0
Printed in the U.S.A. 40 • First printing, January 2000

FLUFFY
MEETS
THE TOOTH FAIRY

by **Kate McMullan**

Illustrated by **Mavis Smith**

Scholastic Reader — Level 3

SCHOLASTIC INC.

New York Toronto London Auckland Sydney
Mexico City New Delhi Hong Kong Buenos Aires

Fluffy's Loose Tooth

"I have a loose tooth, Fluffy,"
said Wade. He wiggled his tooth.
Yikes! thought Fluffy.

"It will fall out," said Wade.

"And I will put it under my pillow. When I am asleep, the tooth fairy will come and take my tooth. And she will leave me a present."

She will? thought Fluffy.

Fluffy liked presents.

He wondered if he had a loose tooth.

He tried to wiggle his right front tooth.

It was not loose.

He tried to wiggle his left front tooth.

It was not loose—or was it?

Maybe it *was* a little bit loose.

Jared came over to Fluffy's cage with
Mr. Lee's class pet, Kiss.
Wade wiggled his tooth for Jared.
"Cool," said Jared. He put Kiss down
in Fluffy's cage.
"My cousin lost her tooth," Jared said.
"The tooth fairy left her a comic book."

I have a loose tooth, Fluffy told Kiss.

You do not, said Kiss.

Yes, I do, said Fluffy.

It will fall out and I will put it under my pillow. The tooth fairy will take my tooth and leave me a present.

Kiss rolled her eyes.

You do not have a pillow, she said.

Wade was doing tricks with his loose tooth. He closed his mouth and made his loose tooth stick out between his lips.
"Gross!" said Jared.

And, Kiss said, **guinea pig teeth**
do not fall out. We gnaw on things
to wear down our teeth.

With his tongue, Wade pulled his tooth
all the way back.

"Yuck," said Jared.

"I can see the insides of your tooth!"

**If we did not gnaw, our teeth
would grow so long we could
not eat,** said Kiss.
Yuck! thought Fluffy.

"Wade!" Jared cried suddenly.
"Your tooth is gone!"

The boys looked on the table
and on the floor.
"You must have swallowed it,"
said Jared.
"Do you think the tooth fairy will
bring me a present?" Wade asked.
Jared shook his head.
"No tooth, no present."

The Lost Lost Tooth

It was Wade's turn to take
Fluffy home for the weekend.
Jared helped Wade carry Fluffy's
cage out to the car.
Wade's sister Zoe sat in the front.
Wade and Fluffy sat in the back.

"Mom! I lost my tooth!" Wade said.
"But I swallowed it. Will the tooth
fairy still leave me a present?"
"Write the tooth fairy a note,"
said Mom, "and put it under your
pillow. The tooth fairy understands
about lost lost teeth."

Zoe turned around in her seat.

"No tooth, no present," she whispered.

Tooth or no tooth, Fluffy hoped the tooth
fairy would leave Wade a present.

That night, Wade wrote a note. He read it to Fluffy:

Dear Tooth Fairy,
My tooth came out today, but I must have swallowed it. So I cannot leave it under my pillow. Can you please leave me a present anyway?

Your friend, Wade

Wade got into his bed and put the note
under his pillow.
"Good night, Fluffy," said Wade.

Fluffy turned around in his hay.
He thought about Wade's tooth.
He hoped Jared and Zoe were wrong about
"no tooth, no present."

Fluffy made himself a fine hole
in the hay and lay down.
Ouch! Something stuck him.
Fluffy jumped up. He dug in the hay.

At last he saw what had stuck him.

Well, well, well, thought Fluffy.
I found the lost lost tooth.

Fluffy Meets the Tooth Fairy

Fluffy squealed and whistled. But he could not wake Wade up.

It's up to me to get this tooth under his pillow, thought Fluffy.

Fluffy turned his food bowl upside down.
He put his cardboard box on top of it.
He put his tunnel on top of that.

Fluffy picked up Wade's tooth and
climbed up, up, up.
At the tip top, Fluffy rocked and wobbled.
Stay cool, pig, thought Fluffy.

Fluffy squeezed his eyes shut.
And down he went.

BOP! He landed on Wade's desk.

He put the tooth in his mouth
and climbed down.

At last Fluffy's feet touched the floor.
All right! he thought. **This pig is
on his way!**
Fluffy was running toward Wade's bed
when he heard a noise.
Is it the tooth fairy? he wondered.

No, it was a cat!

Fluffy hit the ground. He grabbed the
corner of Wade's rug and rolled.

When he stopped, the cat looked in at
Fluffy and Fluffy looked out at the cat.

They looked at each other for a long time.

At last Zoe called, "Brutus! Snack time!"
Brutus zoomed off.
Fluffy rolled the other way.
He rolled himself out of the rug,
and ran to Wade's bed as fast as he could.

Fluffy grabbed a corner of Wade's sheet
and climbed up. And very carefully,
he slipped the tooth under Wade's pillow.
Yes! thought Fluffy. **The pig did it!**

Fluffy was tired. He needed some rest
before he started back to his cage.
He burrowed under the blanket, put his
head on the pillow, and closed his eyes.

The next thing he knew,
the tooth fairy showed up.
**Wow! She looks just like Kiss in
a tutu!** thought Fluffy.
Move it, buddy, she growled. **I can't
lift this pillow with you on it.**

Fluffy jumped up. The tooth fairy lifted
the pillow and grabbed Wade's tooth.
Got it! she cried.
She added it to her necklace made of teeth

I'm out of here, the tooth fairy said.

Hold it! said Fluffy. **What about**

Wade's present?

The tooth fairy rolled her eyes.

Oh, all right, she said.

She pushed two coins under the pillow.

**I put the tooth there. How about a
present for me?** said Fluffy.
It wasn't *your* tooth, she said.
No tooth, no present!

Fluffy rolled off the pillow and woke up.
Was that a bad dream? he wondered.
Just then Fluffy saw something
twinkling above Wade's pillow.
It looked like blue and yellow sparks.
This is a good dream, thought Fluffy.
And he closed his eyes again.

"Fluffy!" Wade called.

Fluffy's eyes popped open.

He was back in his cage.

How had he gotten there?

He had no idea.

"The tooth fairy came!" said Wade.

No kidding, Fluffy thought.

"She left me two quarters!" said Wade.

"And look. She left a present for you."

For me? thought Fluffy.
Wade put a piece of green pepper
into Fluffy's cage.
Fluffy bit into the pepper.
It was sweet and crunchy.

Mmmm, thought Fluffy as he chewed.
No tooth, yes present!